IN THE GHOST DETECTIVE UNIVERSE:

NOVELS
(Best to be read in order)
Beyond the Grave
Unveiling the Past
Beneath the Surface

SHORT STORIES
(All stand-alone)
Just Desserts
Lost Friends
Family Bonds
Common Ground
Till Death
Family History
Heritage
Eternal Bond
New Beginnings
Severed Ties

R.W. WALLACE

Author of *Beyond the Grave*

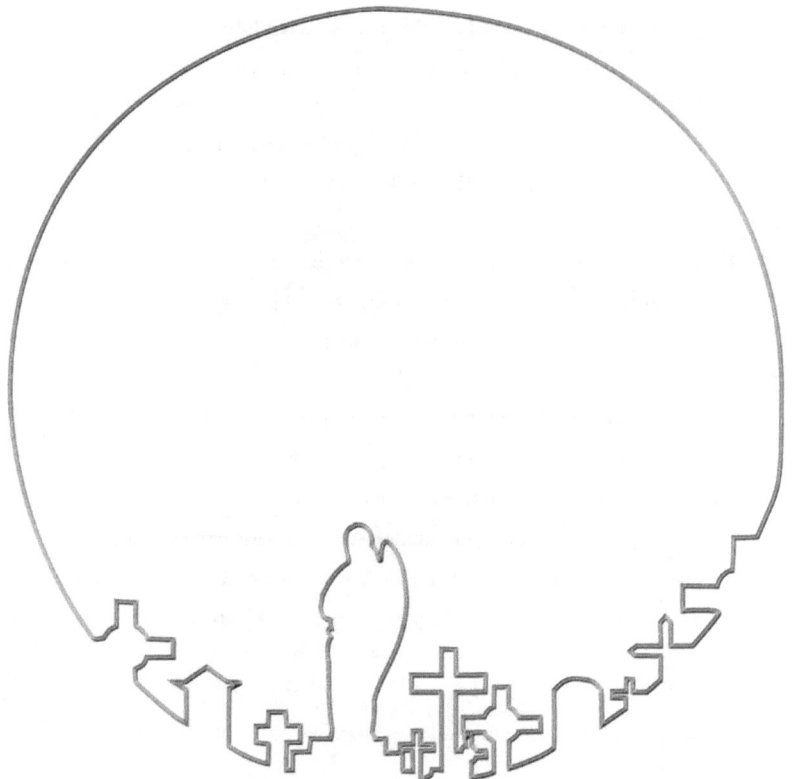

HERITAGE

A Ghost Detective Short Story

Heritage
by R.W. Wallace

Copyright © 2021 by R.W. Wallace

Cover by R.W. Wallace
Cover Illustration 10926765 © germanjames | 123rf.com
Cover Illustration 263199440 © Nouman | Adobe Stock
Cover Illustration 100401076 © gilmanshin | depositphoto.com

This story was first published in *Halloween Harvest*, an anthology edited by Mark Leslie for WMG Publishing

All characters and events in this book, other than those clearly in the public domain, are fictitious and any resemblance to real persons, living or dead, is purely coincidental.

All rights reserved. No part of this publication may be reproduced, distributed, or transmitted in any form or by any means, including photocopying, recording, or other electronic or mechanical methods, without the prior written permission of the publisher, except in the case of brief quotations embodied in critical reviews and certain other noncommercial uses permitted by copyright law. For permission requests, write to the publisher at the address below.

www.rwwallace.com

ISBN paperback: [979-10-95707-95-0]
ISBN ebook: [979-10-95707-96-7]

First edition

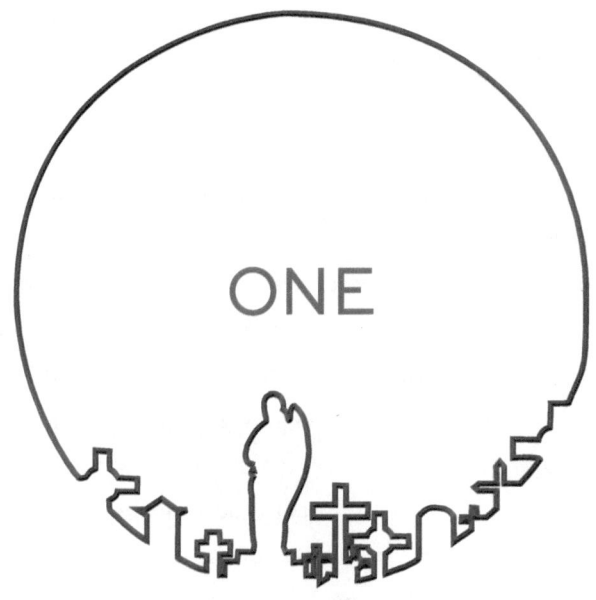

ONE

Please save me from the chrysanthemums. Whoever nicknamed them the daisies of the dead better not come through here or we're going to have words.

I think I remember what they smell like, from long ago, when I still had a physical nose and a sense of smell. Not too sweet, not your typical flower smell. More like an herb, or the smell of fresh dirt.

Which is fitting for a cemetery, I guess.

But it's just too much. All year round our cemetery is monochrome. Most of the tombstones are granite, which can go from the clear gray of a November morning to the dark speckled gray of a starry midnight sky. Some of the older monuments are stone, which is why they're slowly crumbling, leaving the sculpted angels without hands, or with iron spikes sticking out of their wings. The paths are dark gray cobblestones or light gray gravel.

The only color comes from the few cypress trees on the north side of the cemetery and the rare flowers left by mourners. Mostly, the flowers are plastic.

But for two days a year, our cemetery turns into a loud rainbow. Blue, red, white, yellow, orange…you name a color, I can guarantee someone will find a corresponding chrysanthemum.

And they'll cover the family graves with them, and by cover, I mean *cover*. The Cordonnier family down by the well have a classic flat monument with a sober headstone showing names and dates of the deceased. On the Day of the Dead, you cannot even see the color of the monument and just barely make out the top of the headstone through the flowers. This year it's all blue.

The Perrots have opted for red and yellow and they've set the chrysanthemums up in the shape of a cross, one big enough to take on a life-size Jesus.

Not all cemeteries get this much attention, but this particular village seems to have gone a little crazy at one point in history and now can't figure out how to get back to normal. I guess if everybody else's grave is covered in colorful flowers, you don't want to be the *one* family who neglects to come pay your respects to the dead.

Clothilde and I, of course, *have* the two graves where nobody ever places any flowers. Well, Clothilde does, anyway. I don't even have a tombstone to mark the place I'm buried.

Clothilde's last resting place is marked by a simple slab of local white-and-gray granite—the cheapest one available, if I'm not mistaken—and a classic headstone with only her first name and date of death.

The woman herself is now perching on her headstone, her hands under her jeans-clad thighs and her Converse-clad feet gliding through the granite as she swings her feet back and forth. Clothilde has been a ghost for long enough to master the art of deciding which rules of the world of the living to follow. Having a stone to sit on: yes. Having it stop her from dangling her legs: nope.

Her intelligent eyes sweep the cemetery as she shakes her head. "Can't we try telling them they're here on the wrong day? Maybe one of them is sensitive enough to listen?"

"And you think the rest of these crazy people will listen in turn?"

We have this discussion every year. Being ghosts stuck in a cemetery for almost thirty years, we have time to spare, of course, but we're not going to come to any transcending conclusions today either.

In France, the first of November—today—is Toussaint, the All Saints' Day. The second of November is the Day of the Dead, when you're supposed to go to the cemetery to honor the dead and pray for their redemption. The problem is that the first is a public holiday and the second isn't. So little by little, the tradition of coming to the cemetery—with chrysanthemums—has moved over to the first.

"Even if they did hear us," I say to Clothilde from my spot sitting cross-legged on the little bump next to her grave that marks my spot, "it would just mean that they show up a day later. They'd still come at some point. We'd still be flooded with the flowers."

"It *would* be better," Clothilde grumbles. "The people who work tomorrow wouldn't be able to come."

"And a bunch of dead people wouldn't get visits from their families, wouldn't have prayers said for them."

Clothilde rolls her eyes in true teenager fashion. "They don't care. They're dead. And not ghosts. Not anymore, anyway."

Clothilde and I have made it our mission to help the ghosts who come through our cemetery to move on. We don't know where they go—obviously, since we're still here ourselves—but we're convinced it's a better place.

Not everyone becomes a ghost, only the people with unfinished business. It can be as simple as not having said goodbye to a loved one, not having apologized for that one regretful act, or it can be needing justice when someone is murdered and the killer isn't caught.

Solving murders from within the confines of a cemetery when nobody can see or hear you is something of a challenge, but we manage. So far, everybody coming through here as a ghost has moved on.

Except for the two of us, of course.

"The mom at the Tessier grave is here," Clothilde says, tilting her head toward the section with the most recent graves. "She brought roses again."

I stand up to have a better look. The woman buried her son here about six months ago and we've been seeing her every week, without fail.

Can't say I blame her. No parent should ever have to bury their child and the younger they were when they passed away, the worse it is. Daniel Tessier had just turned eighteen.

He never became a ghost, though. So he didn't have any unfinished business. But it seems like his mom does. Not that we know what it is because the woman never speaks. She just sits there, kneeling at her son's grave, staring at his name on the headstone.

"I'm going over to check on her," I say.

Clothilde sighs but jumps down from her perch to follow. "You're not going to get her to talk just because it's the Day of the Dead. Because it's *not* the Day of the Dead. It's All Saints' Day!" She yells the last part across the cemetery.

She gets no reaction from the living, of course.

As we reach her, Madame Tessier is running her fingers over the bright red petals of the roses she brought for her son's grave. Her gaze keeps shifting between the roses and the yellow and orange chrysanthemums of the neighboring grave. Did she not know about the tradition?

"The roses are lovely," I tell her. "A welcome change for those of us who live here."

She doesn't hear me, of course. They never do. But from time to time, we get visitors who are more sensitive to ghosts than most and we can influence them in small ways. Give them ideas that they'll think were their own. Make their skin crawl with the feeling that someone's watching.

That particular feature hasn't actually come in handy to solve any cases. But when she's in the right mood, Clothilde has some fun with it.

Madame Tessier seems more upset than I'd consider normal at the fact that she didn't bring the right type of flowers. She sits back on her heels and looks around the cemetery—probably really seeing the rest of it for the first time—taking in the explosion of color.

"Why is she crying about the flowers?" Clothilde squats down on her haunches to study the woman's face from up close. "There's nothing wrong with your roses, Madame. They're lovely. And probably smell a lot better than that other crap."

Two lonely tears are indeed making their way down the woman's cheeks.

I spot another woman, one I can't remember seeing before, just two graves down. She has put a large pot of purple flowers—yes, yes, chrysanthemums, what else—on the grave of Monsieur and Madame Bartoli. Given their ages and hers, I guess she *might* be a daughter or niece.

Since the woman at the Bartoli grave is already sending worried glances at Madame Tessier, I walk over and talk directly into her ear. "You should go over and tell her that the roses are lovely. She looks like she might need a hug."

Clothilde seems to have come to the same conclusion. She's caressing Madame Tessier's cheek, attempting to swipe the tears away. For a tough-as-nails teenager with a constant I-don't-care attitude, this show of affection is startling.

The Bartoli woman seems to have heard me, bless her. She walks over to the Tessier grave and clears her throat. "Lovely roses," she says in a soft tone. She takes in the dates on the headstone and the picture of a young man next to it. "I'm sorry for your loss, Madame."

Madame Tessier twitches as if brought back to reality. She wipes a hand over her cheek to bat away the tears, hitting Clothilde through the head while she's at it. "Thank you," she says in a wavering voice. "I, uh…I didn't realize today was special." She waves a hand at the rest of the colorful cemetery. "I'm not… not from around here."

The Bartoli woman smiles serenely. "Today is special for the dead who are mostly forgotten the rest of the year. Do not feel guilty for thinking of your lost ones more often than when tradition dictates."

Madame Tessier sighs and sinks lower on her heels. Little by little the air seems to be going out of her and I just hope she'll have the energy to get home safely when she's finished communing with her son.

"My daughter just turned sixteen," the Bartoli woman says.

Her eyes on the picture of her son, Madame Tessier just nods. "He's not here," she says after a while.

"Who?"

"My son. They say he's buried here but I don't believe it. I can't feel him at all. I don't think the body they found in that incinerated dumpster was his."

Clothilde jumps up on the neighboring headstone to perch there. "Well, she's not wrong about him not being here. We never saw the guy."

I can't remember seeing this before. We've had lots of ghosts who want to communicate and reach out to the living but not the other way around. And certainly not when the deceased didn't even become a ghost.

The Bartoli woman doesn't seem to know what to say after that and silently slips away toward the parking lot.

Madame Tessier stays at her son's grave until all the other families have left and the security guard accompanies her to the gate. She never says a word.

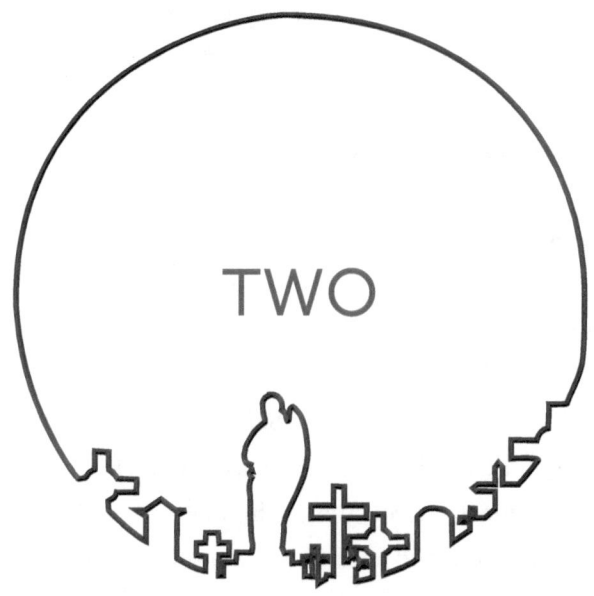

TWO

THAT NIGHT, WE get something new.

In the past few years, we've seen kids getting dressed up and going door to door trick-or-treating. Back when I was alive in the eighties, this wasn't part of the Toussaint celebration in France but something we heard about from across the Atlantic. Now the tradition seems to be inserting itself into French society as well.

In the afternoon, we see the kids with their sugar. At night, it's the teenagers and students—with their alcohol.

My inner police officer winces every time I see these groups. They're drinking too much, wearing too little clothing, not always making sure nobody's left behind. I once saw a girl who couldn't be more than sixteen stagger down the street running along the south wall of the cemetery, wearing nothing but what appeared to be a bloody nurse's uniform with a *lot* of pieces missing and clearly not in a state to take herself home. I wanted to help her, I wanted to call someone who could actually help, I wanted to yell at her friends for abandoning her.

But as a ghost I couldn't do any of those things.

Tonight, it seems like someone wanted to up the stakes. At five minutes past midnight, a witch's hat appears over the south wall, in the spot where the ivy covers it completely, quickly followed by the rest of the witch. She's wearing all black, has long dark hair and enough makeup to make her look seventy instead of probably-nineteen. She jumps the wall and lands on our side with a little squeak and a stumble—yep, she's drunk.

"It's all clear!" she whisper-yells across the wall.

"What the hell is going on?" Clothilde asks. We're standing on the Jacquier family tomb, watching the new arrivals. "Who breaks into a cemetery at midnight?"

"Someone who wants an extra thrill on the Night of the Dead."

Three more heads appear over the wall and with various levels of expertise draw themselves over the wall and through the ivy, to land next to the witch. We have one nun with fake blood pouring out of a slit throat, one zombie who's either very good at imitating the walk of a zombie or very drunk, and one—

"Is that girl dressed as a garden gnome?"

Baggy dark clothing, a red fluffy cap, huge fake beard, large black combat boots, and a heavy backpack. "That…uh…yeah, maybe weird garden gnome."

The gnome seems to be in charge. "All right," she says in a voice tense with excitement. "Let's split up. Whoever starts running or screaming first loses. Selfies in front of at least six graves from different parts of the cemetery. And make it look good and scary, yeah?"

The zombie, who's listing at a fifteen-degree angle, pats himself down, I assume in search of a phone. He ends up finding it in a back pocket and takes an inordinate amount of time to extricate it. "Goddit," he slurs. And ambles off in direction of the church.

The nun and the witch exchange a glance. "Let's start down there?" The nun nods her head in the exact opposite direction of where the zombie went.

"Nuh-huh." The gnome adjusts her backpack and I can hear the clinking of glass. Is she carrying the alcohol of the entire group in there? "We go separately. Otherwise it won't be as scary. And we won't see any ghosts."

Clothilde chuckles. "They want to see ghosts, do they?" Her eyes gleam with anticipated glee. "Can I play? Please, Robert, can I play?"

I can't decide what to think of the situation. The idea of teenagers coming into a cemetery at midnight in the search of ghosts feels…ludicrous. Who still believes in ghosts at that age?

Then again…there *are* actually two ghosts here and we're most definitely real.

And the idea of messing with the kids—because, of course, they don't actually believe in ghosts, they just want to give themselves a good scare—is quite tempting.

"Okay," I tell Clothilde. "We'll follow them around and see what opportunities come up. But no scaring so somebody actually gets hurt, you hear me?"

Predictably, Clothilde rolls her eyes. "Yes, *Dad*."

There's a short argument between the three girls, but the gnome ends up getting her way. They split up, each going toward a different part of the cemetery.

"I wanna mess with the nun," Clothilde says, and takes off after the girl in question.

I'm more intrigued by the gnome, so I decide to follow her. She seems to be a lot less drunk than her friends but still clearly the instigator of this nightly outing. She's also *not at all* looking for ghosts. She walks past looming mausoleums without so much as a glance inside, doesn't spare a second thought to the rotting iron door that's squeaking on its hinges in tonight's slight breeze, and barely even notices the stone angel with only half a head and skeletal wings that people tend to stay away from even in broad daylight.

This girl in on a mission.

Her head *does* whip around when a scream sounds across the cemetery. It's followed by loud cackling but I'm the only one who can hear it—I'd recognize Clothilde anywhere. Guess she managed to give the nun a good scare.

"Seriously?" the gnome girl mutters, hitches her backpack higher on her shoulders, and keeps going. When she passes the Beauvois chapel, her clear eyes dart inside.

I'll admit to considering the possibility of doing like Clothilde and playing with the girl—until I remember I'm a grown man and a police officer to boot. Spooking kids in a cemetery really should be beneath me.

The gnome girl comes to a stop—in front of the Tessier grave.

She dumps her backpack on the ground and opens it to pull out a *shovel* of all things. Please tell me she's not going to vandalize the grave of the poor Tessier boy. The mother has suffered enough as it is.

She walks around the grave with the shovel, studying the granite and the ground around it. She definitely wants in. Why?

After two rounds, she gives up. There's no way for a person to get into that grave without some serious tools. A small spade certainly isn't going to do the trick.

So she starts branching out. Leaving the backpack at the Tessier grave, she ambles past the neighboring graves, looking into the ones with chapels, going behind the large ones, apparently hoping for a hidden entrance.

Then she gets to the newest grave. The one that doesn't host a casket or a body yet.

We don't know who's coming, of course, but *someone* died recently and their grave is being readied. They came in two days ago to dig the hole and I expect the funeral to take place within the week.

Another scream pierces the night. This time it's definitely male and coming from a different part of the cemetery. Clothilde has decided to have fun with all of them.

The gnome girl looks up and frowns in direction of the scream but doesn't stay distracted for long. She seems happy with the empty grave. She goes to get her backpack and proceeds to empty it.

First three empty beer bottles. Then several heavy black plastic bags.

"What you got in there, little gnome?" I ask her. I'm not liking the looks of this.

A flash goes off somewhere nearby. I think I see the witch girl over by the scary angel statue—she's working on their selfie challenge. Clothilde is standing right next to her—a shame she won't show up in the picture—talking into the girl's ear but from the lack of reaction, I'm guessing this girl isn't sensitive to supernatural activities at all.

The gnome girl stays perfectly still, crouching by the open grave, and waits for her friend to move on. When she's alone, she dumps the contents of one of the plastic bags on the ground.

It's a leg.

THREE

I STAND FROZEN in shock as the girl lumps the leg into the open grave and proceeds to do the same with the contents of the remaining bags. I count two lower legs with feet—I'd say male from the size and body hair—two thighs, and two arms.

Something seems off about them at first. As I take a closer look, I realize they're frozen. They're not as soft and malleable as I'd expect skin and flesh to be. These legs and arms were in a freezer not so long ago.

I try to get a better look at the girl, as if seeing her facial features clearly will allow this situation to make more sense. She's white, she has blond hair, but I don't know if it's short or long because of the beanie, and the eyes seem clear though I can't determine the exact color in the dark. Most of her face is covered by the fake beard so I can't even tell the general shape of her face.

When she starts shoveling dirt into the grave to cover the body parts, I run to get Clothilde. She's standing over a cowering nun at the foot of one of the cypress trees, a faintly regretful expression on her pretty face.

"I may have gone too far with this one," she says. "I'm trying to tell her I'm not dangerous and that she's safe here but it's not working as well as the scary stuff."

"Just leave her alone and she'll be fine," I say. "I need you to come with me."

A quick glance at my face and she doesn't even question me. Clothilde *can* be serious when necessary.

When we reach the open grave, the gnome girl has finished covering up the body parts and has shoved the empty plastic bags into her backpack. She's posing for a selfie in front of one of the neighboring graves, wearing a smile that the circumstances make scary as hell.

"She just dumped a pair of arms and legs into that open grave," I tell Clothilde. "This *teenager* killed some guy and is getting rid of the body in our cemetery."

Clothilde jumps into the grave to have a look. As a ghost, she can't dig in the dirt but it seems not all the parts are completely covered. "That's a man's *foot*," she says. I think it's the first time I see my friend genuinely shocked.

The gnome girl finishes taking her pictures and I watch over her shoulder as she sends messages to her friends that it's time to meet up at the spot where they came over the wall.

Then she walks over to the open grave. The venom in her voice surprises me as she says to the buried body parts, "Now you stay here, you hear me?"

I exchange a look with Clothilde. "Interesting."

FOUR

She comes back twice during the night—without her friends but with the gnome outfit still on—first with the upper part of the torso, then with the rest and the head.

"It's that Tessier boy, isn't it?" Clothilde says calmly as she studies the head before it's covered with dirt.

"Seems likely," I reply. "That's where she originally wanted to bury him." We've both been down in the grave since the girl's second trip in a vain attempt to accompany this poor soul during his below-par funeral.

"What is this dump?" I nearly jump out of my nonexistent skin when the angry male voice speaks. "You're not going to leave me here. You're not getting away with this."

"This time you're staying," the gnome girl says through gritted teeth as she shovels more dirt into the hole. "You're not going to bother me ever again."

Clothilde and I hurry out of the grave, me pretending there are stairs to step on and Clothilde not bothering and floating up like a proper ghost. There, leaning over the gnome girl, is the ghost of a young man, his face contorted in anger as he's hissing insults in her ear.

"*Is* that the Tessier boy?"

"I think so," I say. Though it's difficult to link the features of this angry ghost with those of the innocent-looking boy in the picture on the Tessier grave.

The gnome girl can clearly hear the ghost on a certain level because she flinches when he yells at her or touches her, but she keeps working, keeps focused on her task.

"Shouldn't we stop him?" Clothilde asks. "I'm not above a little poking now and then but this guy is too much."

"I'm pretty sure she's the one who killed him, which is why he's a ghost and she's getting rid of his body in a cemetery in the middle of the night."

"Oh. Right." Clothilde cocks her head. "Should we help *him*?"

I shake my head. "I don't like the way he's behaving either. Something's not adding up. We'll talk to him when she leaves."

"But what if he leaves with her?"

I wave at the body parts scattered in the open grave. "His entire body is here now. He's going to be as stuck within these walls as we are. I wonder how the girl figured out this would be the right way to get rid of him."

We never get the chance to know. When she has covered the bottom of the grave with enough dirt and gravel for it to look approximately as even as it was earlier, she grabs her tools and practically sprints to the ivy-covered wall.

Ghost boy sprints after her—I notice he's fresh enough to reflexively follow the rules of the physical realm rather than just flying after her—yelling all the way.

Like I predicted, he's unable to follow over the wall.

"Should we go talk to him?" Clothilde asks as we stand there looking at the boy yelling insults at the gnome girl, at the wall, at the universe.

"Let's give him a couple of minutes to calm down first."

FIVE

It takes him a couple of hours but in the end he calms down enough for us to approach him.

"Good evening, young man," I say to him and have the satisfaction of seeing him jump in fright. "Welcome to our cemetery."

The poor guy shimmers for a few seconds, to the point where I can see straight through him. "You…you're ghosts?"

I look down at myself and at Clothilde. We're all shades of gray without a speck of color. We're not really transparent but also not solid. Clothilde has jumped up to perch on the wall and is dangling her feet through the wall as per usual. "Yes," I reply, just to make sure we don't lose more time than necessary. "We're ghosts. As are you. I'm Robert and this is Clothilde."

At first he just stands there, his mouth hanging open. Then he snaps out of it. "Nathan," he says. "Nathan Tessier."

"Ah, yes. We've met your mother."

"You—you have? My mom's dead?" He suddenly looks five years younger and completely lost.

"No! She's alive and well, I assure you. But she comes to visit your grave quite often."

"My *grave*? My body was just dumped at the bottom of a hole that I'm pretty sure was never meant for me."

"Oh. Right." I turn to look in the direction of the Tessier grave and scratch my head, not that I can feel it. "I wonder whose body is in there." Probably some poor homeless person who was in the wrong place at the wrong time.

Clothilde snorts, followed by an "Oops" and then a "Sorry" in Nathan's direction.

We show Nathan the Tessier grave, with his name and photo and the latest batch of roses. Nathan notices that all the other graves have different flowers and runs his hand through the red petals. "She always loved red roses." Shaking his head, he turns to me. "How long has this been here?"

I point to the date on the headstone. "About six months. Your mother comes by at least once a week. Earlier today she claimed she couldn't feel you here, that you weren't in that grave. Which I find interesting, considering."

"How did you die?" Clothilde asks.

"How did I—?" I can see the anger rising in him like a tidal wave. "That—that—" He points a shaking hand in direction of the ivy-covered wall.

"The gnome girl," I offer.

He snorts a laugh, and his anger recedes just enough for him to find words. "She hit me over the head with a bottle! She *killed* me. Then she shoved my entire body into an empty freezer she had in the basement and left me there for *months*."

"Is that where you became a ghost?" Clothilde says. "Instead of rising from a casket, you rose from a freezer?"

Nathan shrugs. "At first I was stuck in there, but at some point I could get out of the freezer but was still stuck in the house."

"Which is when you started to haunt gnome girl." No wonder she needed to get rid of him.

"Well…yeah. What else was I supposed to do?"

Good point.

"She just hit you over the head with a bottle? For no reason?" Clothilde paces by the neighboring grave. I'm guessing she wants to sit on it but doesn't want to get too close to the chrysanthemums.

"Well…yeah."

I use the oldest questioning technique in the book: silence.

And it works like a charm. "I mean, we were having an argument, all right? We were both really angry, and then, bam! I'm dead."

"Mhmm." Clothilde eyes our new arrival, sizing him up. He's taller than me and seems to be in good shape. The gnome girl wasn't exactly weak—she managed to carry this guy's body here, after all—but she was quite small.

"What were you arguing about?" I ask him.

He huffs. "You know. Couple's stuff."

Clothilde's eyebrows shoot up. "She was your *girlfriend*?"

"She was until five minutes before I died."

SIX

WE DON'T GET anything else out of him for the rest of the night. We go back to Clothilde's grave and let Nathan take in the site of his own tombstone in peace.

The next day, the actual Day of the Dead, his mother returns.

The weather is as gray and sad as yesterday, with the breeze having picked up some speed and heavy clouds in the west promising rain in the near future. Nathan's mother is wearing her usual jeans and black sneakers, with a dark purple raincoat.

She brings a pot of yellow chrysanthemums.

"Mom!" Nathan says when she arrives at his grave.

Madame Tessier, who hasn't reacted at all when we've tried

talking to her during her visits, who I would have declared as completely insensitive to ghosts, turns her head in her son's direction. "Nathan?"

"Oh shit," Clothilde says. We've approached to observe but keep out of the conversation, at least for the moment. And there *is* a conversation, which is astounding.

"Mom, you have to help me. You have to get Mélanie. She *killed* me, Mom. She put me in the freezer and cut my body into pieces and now dumped me *here*. She can't get away with it, Mom."

Tears are forming in Madame Tessier's eyes. "I'm so happy you're finally here, Nathan. I was worried I wouldn't be able to help you find peace."

"Huh," I say. "Looks like we're getting help this time."

"What do you think he needs to move on?" Clothilde asks.

"Murder victims usually need the murderer to be caught."

"Mhmm."

"You have to go find Mélanie," Nathan pleads with his mom. "She used her father's tools to cut up my body and just cleaned them in the bathroom sink before taking them back out to the garage. Get the cops over there today, Mom."

Madame Tessier cocks her head to the side as if trying to make something out. She's the most sensitive person I've ever seen but I don't think she's hearing her son's actual words. It's probably more of a general feeling.

"It was because of Mélanie, wasn't it?" she says finally. The sadness in her tone surprises me. Lowering her head, she says, "I knew I should have left earlier."

Nathan looks about as confused as I feel.

Madame Tessier scans the cemetery. An elderly couple is setting up some flowers on a grave close to the church but otherwise the place is deserted. "I saw the signs," she says with a faraway look in her eyes. "But I didn't act. I was so used to looking the other way and finding excuses that I didn't stop and think what it was doing *to you.*

"When you were kicked out of your first school, I blamed the teachers. They simply didn't know how to channel your energy. When you weren't allowed to continue karate…well, I was too absorbed in healing my own visible wounds to worry about your invisible ones.

"And when you hit that teacher… That's when I realized I had to get us out. But it was already too late, wasn't it?"

"What's she talking about?" Clothilde whispers.

"I'm guessing an abusive husband with anger management issues," I reply.

Nathan seems to be frozen on the spot. He's back to looking twelve instead of eighteen. He's like a lost little boy.

"I'm guessing you hit Mélanie?" Madame Tessier says sadly. She sighs. "Such a sweet girl. But easily distracted, wasn't she? Can probably get annoying fast. For you."

"She never finished a sentence," Nathan whispers. "She'd start one sentence and then finish another one."

Madame Tessier runs a hand over the flowers she brought for her son's grave. "Can't believe that little girl had the guts to do what I never managed." She swallows. "You have to understand that this isn't her fault, *chéri*. Nor is it yours. It's your father's, for teaching you the wrong way to manage your emotions. And mine, for not getting you away soon enough.

"I'm sorry, Nathan. I hope you'll finally find peace now." She pushes the roses from yesterday a little to the side so that they're just below the picture of her son.

And she leaves.

ଓ

I PLAN TO let Nathan be for a while after his mother leaves but when I see him turning translucent I realize he's ready to move on.

"You all right, Nathan?" I ask him as I approach where he's sitting on his own grave running his hands through the roses. "Looks like you've found the closure you needed to move on."

He holds up his hand. It's see-through. "It's not my fault," he says with wonder in his voice. And disappears.

I join Clothilde at the freshly dug grave currently housing the defrosting and dismembered body of Nathan Tessier. "You think we should help someone notice that there's an extra body down there?"

We could. When they come with whoever that grave is for, we should be able to find someone sensitive enough for us to give them the thought that the grave doesn't seem quite as deep as it should be. They'll find the body parts and chances are the young Mélanie didn't cover her tracks well enough and get arrested.

Neither mother nor son seemed to actually need for the girl to get caught to get closure.

"I think just this once, we'll not interfere."

AUTHOR'S NOTE

THANK YOU FOR reading *Heritage*! I wrote this story for an anthology called Halloween Harvest, edited by Mark Leslie for WMG Publishing. For those who don't know Mark, he's a *huge* fan of skeletons and Halloween and therefore the perfect match for this anthology. I was thrilled to be part of it, alongside so many wonderful writers and stories.

Heritage is the seventh Ghost Detective short story I've written. You can find links to all the others (ten at the time of writing this note), and to the series of novels set in the same world with the same characters, in the next pages.

If you want to make sure never to miss a new release, remember you can sign up for my newsletter on rwwallace.com

R.W. Wallace
www.rwwallace.com

Also by R.W. Wallace

Mystery

Ghost Detective Novels
Beyond the Grave
Unveiling the Past
Beneath the Surface

Ghost Detective Shorts
Just Desserts
Lost Friends
Family Bonds
Common Ground
Till Death
Family History
Heritage
Eternal Bond
New Beginnings
Severed Ties

The Tolosa Mystery Series
The Red Brick Haze
The Red Brick Cellars
The Red Brick Basilica

Short Story Collections
Deep Dark Secrets
A Thief in the Night

Time Travel Secrets (short stories)
Moneyline Secrets
Family Secrets

Romance

French Office Romance Series
Flirting in Plain Sight
Hiding in Plain Sight
Loving in Plain Sight

Standalone Novels
Love at First Flight

Holiday Short Stories
Down the Memory Aisle
Morbier Impossible
A Second Chance
The Magic of Sharing
The Case of the Disappearing Gingerbread City
The Lucia Crown
Crooks and Nannies

Young Adult

Short Story Collections
Tales From the Trenches

Find all R.W. Wallace's books:

rwwallace.com/allbooks

ABOUT THE AUTHOR

R.W. WALLACE WRITES in most genres, though she tends to end up in mystery more often than not. Dead bodies keep popping up all over the place whenever she sits down in front of her keyboard.

The stories mostly take place in Norway or France; the country she was born in and the one that has been her home for two decades. Don't ask her why she writes in English—she won't have a sensible answer for you.

Her Ghost Detective short story series appears in *Pulphouse Magazine*, starting in issue #9.

You can find all her books, long and short, all genres, on rwwallace.com.

www.ingramcontent.com/pod-product-compliance
Lightning Source LLC
LaVergne TN
LVHW041716060526
838201LV00043B/774